HIND POCKET BOOKS

Search for Truth

Dr. Sarvepalli Radhakrishnan was the first Vice President of India and went on to become the second Indian President. He was a statesman and a philosopher. Dr. Radhakrishnan was one of the leading scholars of comparative religion and philosophy in his days and helped to bridge the gap between Eastern and Western thought. He introduced Western idealism into Indian philosophy.

Dr. Sarvepalli Radhakrishnan was the first scholar of note to provide a comprehensive interpretation of India's religious and philosophical literature to English-speaking peoples. He became Vice President of India in 1952 and was elected President of India in 1962; he held the office until 1967.

Dr. Radhakrishnan was awarded Bharat Ratna in the year 1954 and his birthday is celebrated every years as Teacher's Day in India on 5 September.

Search for Truth

Dr. Sarvepalli Radhakrishnan

HIND POCKET BOOKS
An imprint of Penguin Random House

HIND POCKET BOOKS

USA | Canada | UK | Ireland | Australia
New Zealand | India | South Africa | China | Singapore

Hind Pocket Books is part of the Penguin Random House group of companies whose addresses can be found at global.penguinrandomhouse.com

Published by Penguin Random House India Pvt. Ltd
4th Floor, Capital Tower 1, MG Road,
Gurugram 122 002, Haryana, India

HIND
POCKET
BOOKS

First published in Hind Pocket Books 2009
This Edition published in 2021

10 9 8 7 6 5 4 3 2

ISBN : 9788193935538

Printed at Repro India Limited

www.penguin.co.in

MIX
Paper from
responsible sources
FSC® C047271
FSC
www.fsc.org

This is a legitimate digitally printed version of the book and therefore might not have certain extra finishing on the cover.

CONTENTS

Search For Truth	2
Seeking The Supreme Reality	13
Quest For Spiritual Freedom	23
Of Knowledge And Action	33
The Divine In Us	41
Essential Values of Culture	49
Fruits of Knowledge	59
Creed of Wisdom And Love	73
Man Has Yet To Grow	83
Touch of The Universal	91
Depth of Life	99
Our Common Heritage	107
Growth of Knowledge And Wisdom	115
Knowledge of The Self	123
Freedom Of The Human Spirit	131
Insight Into Reality	143
Discipline of Spirit	153
Nothing Like Knowledge	161
The Majesty of Law	169
Challenge of Creative Cinema	183
Trustee of Human Vision	193

Search for Truth

Religion, or a search for truth, is a necessity. When we look at the cosmic process, we find things succeeding one another; great civilisations, great embodiments of art — great things arise, spring up and pass away. And we ask the question, 'Is this passing away all or is there anything which does not pass away?' Is there anything which may be regarded as unchanging in this process of incessant change, is a question which every reflective individual is bound to raise. He cannot think that mere annihilation is the end of all existence, that the cosmic process arises and passes away. The question is bound to arise and that is why all the great seekers of truth have raised this question.

The *Upanishad* seer says, Lead me from the

unreal to the real, from darkness to light, from death to immortality'. In other words, he feels that the world in which we happen to exist is one of unreality, darkness and death and he does not want to believe that darkness, death and unreality are the end of all existence. He feels the necessity for something which goes beyond these things and so utters a prayer saying, 'Lead me from that;

Similarly, Buddha raised the question, 'Old age, sickness, death are they all, or is there anything beyond them? Can man emancipate himself from the dominion of time with its characteristics of old age, death and sickness, or is annihilation the last word?'

Similarly, the Christian Gospel says, 'Death is not the end of all. The grave will not have its victory.' The Christian Gospel does not make out the Crucified lord to be the last word. It says, 'He has risen.' That is, there is something which survives death. No individual on earth would be content with this kind of life if it were all. If time were all, if everything is devoured by time and if there is nothing which transcends time, if there is no such thing as eternity, then there can be no meaning in this life.

If life has significance, if it has any meaning, if it has any kind of purpose, we must have something which supersedes time, which is exempt from death, and which makes us feel there is a deathless element in all. If this cosmic process were all, if this existence — existence literally meaning standing out — if that is the thing, what is the reality? The answer comes — the reality must be Being, because if there were no Being there would be no existence, no standing out of it.

Is that Being unintelligent, inert? No. The very order, progress, which you find in this world, indicates to you that it must have some kind of intelligence and purpose. In this world the only possible expression of that Supreme Being which you regard as infinite possibility? Is He obliged to bring out this possibility or has He any freedom in the choice of the stage? So we call it freedom. You may call it *Saccidananda*, being, intelligence and freedom. But these are things which we are called upon to admit or recognise by way of merely ransacking the nature of this world, asking questions — whether this world is all or whether there is anything which underlies it, which informs and animates it, and whether that something has got intelligence and purpose, whether it has the freedom to choose whatever it is, whatever it wishes to bring about.

The real quality of religion is brought out by our incessant search, unceasing quest, for knowing the truth of things and for increasing the objects of compassion we have in this world. Intensity of search and extension of objects to which we apply love, these constitute the two sides of a truly spiritual man. We must always keep up this pursuit of truth until we are able to discover it, see it face to face. And whatever it may be, every human individual has got the same impulse in him and so deserves our love, our consideration. Society, all civilisation, has been one persistent effort to live in harmony with other beings. We maintain this effort. We go on trying until the whole world becomes our own family; our kingdom.

There are statements given in all religions which emphasize this aspect, the spiritual character of man. The four *Vedus* have four *Mahavakyas* which insist on this. The *Vedas* have been reported with a faithfulness which is unparalleled in the history of the literatures of the world.

prajnanambrahma

The intelligence is Divine.

ayamatma brahma

The soul is Divine.

aham brahmasmi

I am Divine.

tattvamasi

That art Thou.

These four Statements, taken from four different Vedas, emphasize the one fundamental truth. And that truth is that man has the capacity to rise beyond the present position, to surpass himself, to fulfil himself. This fulfilment is not merely a vain dream. But it is something which, by effort, will be possible for us to realise. The Christian Gospel tells us the same thing, 'Know you not that you are the temple of God and the spirit of God dwelleth in you? Muhammad tells us that God is nearer to you than the artery of your neck. Every religion says *deho devalayo nama*. The *deha*, the body, must be regarded as *devalaya*, *jiva* which is *sanatana* is something which is eternal in character. If we overlook that spirit, that spark of the divine which we all have, we will become bound to things, ideas and abstractions. We lose the real creativity of the human individual himself.

Unless we are able to withdraw ourselves from the stream of becoming, from the series of events, from all those things which happen one after another, unless we are able to feel that there is some element in us which is trans-objective, which supersedes the mere objective series of happenings, we are not true men. We become a thing. We become an object. We become not a human being, but a de-humanised unit of our society. The essential thing is, whether you are a scientist or a technologist, a philosopher or a dramatist, or whatever you may be, you must realize the living spirit which is in you.

Harvard University has for its motto *Veritas* (truth). Heidelberg University has its motto 'The Living Spirit', the living spirit which is in you of which all things are the expressions, of which science, literature, art, all these are the expression. It is when the human individual is able to withdraw himself into himself and sit in judgement on the things which are presented to him, it is then that he will be able to judge, that he will be able to create.

We have said all these things. But in society we have not applied this doctrine of the sanctity of the individual. No individual should be degraded, no man should be desecrated by poverty, by disease, by ignorance etc. If we are true to the gospel which we announce, our social order must reflect it. But so long as the social order does not reflect it, we are merely talking and are not faithful to the principles which we pronounce.

Lately, there has been a real awakening in this matter, not merely in our country but in all countries. There is a tendency to see to it that racialism, colonialism and such other things are wiped out, that human individuals are freed from political oppression, social degradation, economic exploitation, racial oppression; all these things must be removed. If we really regard the individual as sacred, as dignified, as a spark of spirit, it is essential for us to understand that so long as these things are acquiesced in, we are unfaithful to the fundamental principles of what we profess. Our professions are one thing, our practices are quite different. It is that divorce which has brought us to this present condition and it is that divorce which we should try to overcome if we wish to improve our condition.

Even in international affairs, it is the same matter. For the last two thousand years, there has not been a decade when we did not have military conflicts in this world. And still, today, we are having them. The principle is "resist not evil". The practice is, "resist evil by force if it becomes necessary". This thing is going on in the world. But no God interferes with us. No stars will avail. Even on the Cross at Calvary, God did not come and save Jesus from crucifixion.

There is so much of inequality, so much of injustice, in this world. It is the human individual who has to realise that God is the spark in him. It is he that has to take into account his own creativity, his own freedom. It is possible for the human individual to make this world a better one, because the human individual is the image of the Divine and, therefore, so long as he is doing the right thing, he is progressing, it is possible for him to bring about a better future than the one which we now have.

Standing in the present crisis, when the whole past is vague and dim and the present is so turbulent and the future so intimidating, what is necessary now is for the human individual to realize his own greatness, the concealed greatness in him which he has forgotten, which he has not taken care of, taken account of. Take that and try to apply those canons of spirit to social behaviour and improve the society and see to it that society really reflects the divine order which we think of.

Seeking The Supreme Reality

I have spent more than 50 years of my life in the study of our ancient scriptures and also Western thought. The more I delve into things, the more I am impressed by the unity of aspiration of the human mind, wherever it may be found. We are all interested in finding out the truth of things.

The *Brahma Sutra* starts with the verse, *athato brahmajijnasa.* Now, therefore, the desire to know Brahman. Is there anything in this world? Everything we look upon is perpetually changing. The world seems to be a number of risings and perishings. Is there anything which is unchanging, eternal, in this adventure of time? Simply because we feel the need for it, it does not follow that there is something. We may be hungry, that does not mean that we have food. There must be some reason by which we understand what our yearnings are and whether there is anything to satisfy them.

So, the second *sutra* tells us, *janmady asya yatah*. That from which all beings arise, all beings are sustained, into which they are dissolved, that is the Ultimate Reality. Find out yourself whether such an Ultimate Reality is or is not, by rational means, by investigation, by *jijnasa*, by *alocana*. We try to find out whether there is anything answering to this Supreme Reality. *Janmady asya yatah takes its stand on the Taittriya Upanisad — yato va imani bhutani jayante, yena jatanti jivanti, yat prayantyabhisamvisanti, tad vijijnasasva; tad brahmeti, sa tapo'tapyata, sa tapas taptva.*

When he makes out that tapas is brahma, he is making out that the very aspiration that we have is indicative of the Reality. When he makes out that tapas is brahma, he makes out that the longing which we have, the yearning which we have, is itself symptomatic of the woking of the Supreme in our minds and hearts. If it were not there, you would not havc it, you would not ask for it. So the Taittiriya Upanisad tells us that if you look at the world and if you look at the successive stages through which it has come to its present position — anna, prana, manas, vijnana and ananda — you will scc that this world is progressing, unfolding and registering all the progressive values.

Therefore, by rational means, by investigation, by looking upon the world and asking question whether this world is self-sustaining, or whether there is anything else behind it, informing and animating it, we get the answer that there is that Ultimate Reality. But if this is inferential, we are merely getting this answer by way of logical reasoning. There is always a difference between textual learning, logical reasoning and personal encounter with the Absolute Reality.

So, the third *sutra says, sastra-yonitvat.*

The *sastras* register the personal experiences of all the great sages and saints. You cannot understand the Reality merely by logic. You must be able to say, "I have felt that Reality." It is not merely a question of logical speculation. It is a question of personal encounter. Such personal encounters are registered in the scriptures.

We find in the *Nyayasutra* that the *Veda* is *aptavacana*. But who are the aptas? All those who have *brahmaprapti* are the aptas; those who have realisation of God, they are the *aptas*. Their words, their sayings, are registered in the scriptures themselves. *Vakyartha jnanamatrat na amrtam*. We cannot get that Reality, that personal satisfaction; that is what has been said by *Vedanta Desika*.

We cannot get real salvation in our own life if we are merely thinking about and speculating about Reality. We must be in a position to say, "I have seen God, I have seen *Brahma*, I have known that it is there working in everyone's mind." That is *sastra* and that is apta-vacana.

Aptas are not confined to our country alone, rsi arya mlecchanam *samanam laksanam*. This brahma-prapti, this God-realisation, is something which is found wherever there are aspiring souls, wherever there are seeking minds, wherever there are people who are hungry for truth and eager for seeing the Absolute Reality.

But then, these statements conflict with one another. The sastras do not all point in the same direction. We have a large number of contradictory statements. So the fourth verse says, *tat tu sananvayat.* Reconciliation of all these statements will have to be made, and reconciliation of all these statements is possible.

Knowledge cannot be divided against itself. it must point out to us that the scientific knowledge, or metaphysical knowledge, or religious truth, all must indicate in the same way. *Sarva sastra prayojanam atma darsanam*. Whether in science or technology, or humanities or arts, whatever you may study, if you study then sufficiently deeply, you will find out that they all indicate that three is a living spirit in us. *Antaryami brahma* is in us.

The *mahavakyas* indicate that the Supreme dwells in man. He is not somewhere in the sky, He is not somewhere up above. He is here within us. If you search deeply, you will find Him. If we penetrate behind the layers of our body, mind and intellect, we will find there the quick of consciousness, the flame of consciousness, *jyotisam jyotih*, from which all things come.

You will find, therefore, that what our ancient scriptures have said must be regarded as something which is tenable even today. There is nothing which is irrelevant, or which is invalid. You can question it by logic, by light. You will find out that the truths are there. That is the greatness of our literature, of our religious literature. Our classics are for all time. There is nobody who will say that these things which the first four *sutras* of the *Brabma Sutra* enunciate are anything intangible or imponderable. Man must enquire, must use his reason, must discipline his mind and heart, so that what he arrives at is reasonable conclusion, is seen by him as reality face to face; and then the contradictions, if any, among the *sastras* can be easily reconciled.

Quest For Spiritual Freedom

The world suffering from scepticism in faith, anarchy in morals; and we do not know which way to turn and what to do. In spite of our striking and spectacular achievements of science and technology, there is a deep void in the minds of men. They do not know how to fill that void. Because people today are cultivated in methods of science, they would like to have a spirit of enquiry encouraged in them and we must present to them certain things which will appeal to their conscience — intellectual and moral. We cannot present any faith which is not rooted in reason. Everyone asks us, is this a rational faith, the faith that enquires, that what we should have; and is it possible for us to attain the goal of religion by means which are commendable to reason and conscience?

So far as our country is concerned, we have insisted on all these aspects. The Bhagavadgita itself in its colophon say: *brahmavidyayam yogasastre srikrsnarjuna-samvade*. Brahmavidya is an intellectual enquiry, a rational investigation. We want to find out what this world is about. That is what you call *brahmavidya. Yogasastra* is what is called practical discipline, which will convert an intellectual proposition into a life conviction. *Krsnarjunasamvada* is the meeting of the individual soul with the Supreme Soul. That is the end, the goal, the fulfilment. If you ask what is *brahmavidya*, it is referred to in a chapter, *Bhrguvidya*, in *Taittiriya Upanisad*.

bhrgur vai varunih varunam upasasara, adhihi bhagavo brahmeti

That is how it starts, Bhrgu asks his father, Varuna, to tell him what is brahma. Father answers:

yato va imani bhutani jayante,

yena jatami jivanti yat prayanty abbisamvisanti, tad vijijnasasva, tad brahmeti

so tapo' tapyata, sa tapas taptva

You must try to find out that reality, which is comprehensive and coherent, that category which accounts for every aspect of the universe, that is what he says, all things that are born, that by which they are sustained, into which they are dissolved. Is there anything which is so comprehensive and which coherently includes all these things? That is the question which is asked. He says, you have to learn it by *tapas*; then answers, *tapobrahma:* if you perform *tapas,* that very aspiration is due to a stirring of the divine in you; because you have the divine in you, you ask for an explanation, otherwise you would never ask for it. Therefore, he says, *tapobrahma* and *brahmavijijnasasva*, by tapas you will find what it is. Tapa, according to Panini, is *alocana,* reflection. It is getting into the second thoughts, not merely being satisfied with the first appearances of a thing but to go behind them. That is what *tapas* is.

If you exert that way, you get an answer that this whole universe cannot be regarded as merely a chance occurrence, it is not an accidental rising up. It is not something which is to be regarded as a freak: it enables you to see that there is a progressive unfolding of values: you start with matter, come to life, start with life and come to mind, and from mind you come to intelligence. Intelligence is also disturbed by doubts and other things. So you get tranquillity of spirit, what is called supreme *ananda*.

Spiritual freedom is at the root of this universe and from that freedom, intelligence, mind, life, matter, all arise. That is very good. Explanation is good, because we understand it. It is not dogmatic, it is not due to any assertion of any sage or anybody. It is a matter of our looking at the panorama of the universe and trying to find out what it is that exactly accounts for. After *brahmavidya* you have *yogasastra.* Mere *brahmavidya* will not do. Mere intellectual knowledge does not make you into a spiritual being.

Science looks at the periphery of the world, the outside of things, the variety and the multiplicity of the universe, but the centre of the being from which all these things come, from which they arise, that must be felt only by solitary meditation. It is not by intellectual discourse that you can have it, but you have to take away your mind, abstract it, so to say, detach it from the occurrences of the world and concentrate on the centre of the being and try to understand what the structure of the Ultimate Reality is. By *vakyarthajnana* — by textual learning — you cannot get eternal bliss. So it is *yogasastra.* If you discipline yourself, if you get rid of anger, hatred, pusillanimity, pettiness, when you deal with people, you see God face to face. 'Blessed are the pure in heart for they shall see God.' If you are able to purify your heart, if your are able to cleanse it; so to say, if you are able to completely rid your mind of every kind of egoistic selfishness, you see God even as Arjuna saw *Krsna*. It is *krsna-rjunasamvada*. It is a communion of the individual soul with the Supreme Soul.

You have, therefore, a philosophy and a religion which asks you to enquire, which asks you to convert the result of enquiry into a burning conviction of your own, and then, when you become transparent, so to say, when there is nothing selfish in you, egoistic in you, when your heart becomes purified, you will see God; the Ultimate Reality is perceived by you through the pulse of your being; it is not what another man says, it is what you see with your own eyes, feel with your heart and feel in the pulse of your being. A philosophy like that which asks you to enquire, to discipline yourself and then tells that you will attain the goal of religion. It is seeing God face to face. It is a religion like that which will have vogue in the world hereafter.

I have been in different parts of the world and I have seen growing scepticism and the way in which they tell us, 'please use your reason and tell us if there is any reality in this world.' There is no eclipse of God. But God is revealed as the fundamental reality standing behind and before all this universe and it is He that is responsible for the gradual unfolding of supreme values, which we cherish as fundamental to our culture.

Of Knowledge And Action

In this country, we have had a long tradition where education and service always went together. In the famous *Mundaka Upanisad* it is said:

atmah-krida atma-ratih, kriyavan esa brahma-vidam varisthah

The man who delights in the self, sports in the self and performs work *kriyavan*, he is to be regarded as the best of knowers of *Brahman*.

In other words, performance of work without any sense of compulsion or duress, for the mere pleasure of serving humanity, is the highest kind of service. That is why the *Bhagavadgita* concludes by saying; the yoga of Krsna must be combined with the *dhanus* of Arjuna; that is, practical efficiency and theoretical understanding of what you attempt to do and the practical work which you do. The *dhanus* of Arjuna symbolises the actual work: the yoga of *Krsna* symbolises the contemplation which is essential before any work is done. But, in our times, we do first and then think, but there it is said that we must first think and then act. A Western philosopher, Whitehead, said: 'we build Cathedrals in our mind first before we build them up outside.' We first of all contemplate what we wish to do and then realize it in action. There is a famous verse which tells us that we have had great philosopher statesmen in this world.

> *viveki sarvada muktah kurvato nasti karta alepa-vadam asritya Sri Krsna Janakau yatha*

Sri *Krsna* and Janaka were great knowers, seers and also doers; so the tradition of combining knowledge with work has been an ancient one, coming from the time of the *Upanisads* down to our own age.

Plato is not the first to tell us about it. We have had some ideas about this matter. One of our ancient seers said: 'The best life one can have is the life in the company of great books and great men'. A university can give you great books, but it must also give great men.

There are books for all time. There are books for our time. We should try to understand the books for all time, the classics, their lessons are all-pervading, are eternal in their value. It is better to suffer ourselves than inflict suffering on others. It is an eternal truth. It is not a truth for our times. There are books which tell us about these things. There are others which tell us only about the planning for the present, what we should do in the next five years. They are of interest; but they are not of the same interest as the books for all time. The classics are the contemporaries of all ages; they do not belong merely to our age; they belong to all ages.

It is necessary for our boys and girls to have a proper sense of values. They must have a sense of proportion in the things which they do, "understanding of great books and company of great men." Where are the great men and where are the great books? They are all rusting. But it is no use collecting books. It is necessary to make students love reading. A really educated man, a university man, must be a lover of reading He must be able to understand, he must be able to feel unhappy if he is not doing some real reading in his life. Therefore it is, if you are able to provide our young men and women with proper opportunities for leading good lives, you must make them understand what a good life consists of and what the good men have done. We must try to inculcate this habit of reading in our youngsters. If this habit of reading is not there, the education is wasted, the spirit of youth is wasted on all of them.

We should try to imbibe the valuable lessons

of all cultures. It is necessary for us to produce what is said to be a composite synthesis of the different cultures which flowed into this land. If we are able to do it, the present discords and animosities, which divide man from man, which make this world a hell on earth, these things will be removed soon. But for that also, education in the proper sense is necessary. You may have buildings, you may have books. But they will all be rusting there, unless the students themselves have got the zest to read those book and to profit by them and to feel unhappy when they are not in the company of great books or great souls.

The Divine In Us

What is it that education aims at? YOU have that invocation song: you must make yourself as white, *svachha, dhavala,* then *nihsesa jadyapahah,* all the diseases in your mind will have to be removed. Clarity of speech, purity of body, sanctity of spirit, all these three things are to be aimed at by education.

There are many people who think that India is a nation given to metaphysical reveries and is indifferent to the mundane world and the work of the service of humanity, As a matter of fact, metaphysical fulfilment consists in the development of your body, mind and spirit: *pranaramam mana anandam santi samrddham amrtam. Amrta* or deathlessness is realized here on earth by that quality, *pranaramam*, by the play of your vital life, *mana anandam*, by the satisfaction of your mind, *santi samrddham*, by the abundance of the tranquillity of spirit; if these three things you have, you have attained *moksa* here and now on earth.

It is not necessary for you to pass on to another world to attain *amrta*. If there has been anything which our scriptures have taught us, it is this, *deha* is *devalaya*. Each human being must be regarded as the temple of God. It is *devalaya* and we generally are inclined to forget the pure spirit which is in us and are lost in the trivialities of life. Such people find mental unrest, neurosis and other things. If you overlook the eternal in us, and it is then that we are lost in this world, we do not know what we have to do. We become exiles from ourselves, strangers in this world, so to say. The great Vedas asserted this spiritual quality of man. Their four *mahavakyas* are:

prajnanam brahma

ayamatma brahma

aham brahmasmi

tat vam asi

You are the divine. You are the candidate for divinity. God is not somewhere up in the heaven. He is there in the inward centre of your being. You overlook it, you forget it, you are lost in the peripheral activities, in the trivialities of your life and, therefore, you are exiled from yourself and you feel helpless and that kind of moral helplessness is what characterises many of the so-called educated youth today.

If our educated men are to regard themselves as truly educated, they must be aware of this central being in us from which body, mind and intellect emanate. Deeper down, lower down, by penetrating these outer layers, you are able to discover the nerve and quick of your conscious life, the eternal consciousness from out of which all other activities emanate. If the Vedas proclaimed that every human being has the quality of the divine and has to develop it and if it is said, '*deha* or body is a *devalaya*,' why is it that we have introduced all sorts of artificial and contingent distinctions among men and look upon some men as lower and other men as higher. It is something which is contradictory to the real spirit of our teachings. It is necessary for us to get over all these distinctions and to believe in the humanity of every human being and in the capacity of every human being to rise to the highest stature of his spiritual life. Unless we are able to do it, we are not truly educated, we are *nara pasus,* human animals, who walk about in this world merely feeding ourselves, procreating and then looking after our own interests.

The hunger for power has taken hold of us. It must be hunger for service, service of humanity, making every human individual feel that he has got the potentiality of rising to the very highest. 'Be perfect even as your Father in heaven is perfect.' That divine perfection is something which is within the reach of every one. You are not able to aim at that if you do not aim at the fulfilment of your being, at the true fulfilment of your being. It does not consist in physical growth or material possession or intellectual eminence; it consists in the discovery of the spiritual in you and the spiritual in every other man. The world is to be regarded as a single community of people who have got the same ideals, the same aspirations, the same causes and the same hopes as you happen to possess. It is because we neglected this aspect that we have become a prey to all sorts of ills. If their are mental illness, the sickness of mind from which most of us suffer, it is because we have overlooked the divine in each one of us. It is our duty as truly educated beings to discover that divine, to find out that we have got something more than mere intellect, mind and body, the eternal spirit. In different ways we have emphasised this one spirit; it is because of this, in spite of so many changes and chances in life, all these four to five thousand years, we have survived, we have been able to produce in each generation a few people who incarnate this eternal spirit of India. It is because of that that we still survive and that we are still having ambitions for a progressive future.

You have sciences, you have humanities, you have commerce, you have art; each one of these is to be regarded as an endeavour to enable you to seek the divine in you. Why is it called *KALA? Kam paramatmanam lati grhnati iti kala.* Every *kala* which you absorb is something which enables you to absorb or to grasp the Eternal. The Eternal is not somewhere up above. It is here in the temporal; the temporal and the eternal, the sacred and the secular, are bound up one with another. There is no such thing as a divorce between the two. So, whatever work we do, we have to do it as many times as it has been repeated: *bahu jana hitaya, bahu jana sukhaya.*

ESSENTIAL VALUES OF CULTURE

Literature has been with us from the beginning of our history. Literature should satisfy two standards — attain artistic excellence and serve the interest of humanity. It must have a sense of beauty and it must also serve the interest of humanity. Beauty and humanism, diese are the two defining characteristics of any kind of literature. Our country, which is a vast one with a long history, has been multi-lingual from the very start. We have had many languages in which great literatures have been produced. But the one essential idea has been to bring languages and peoples, races, cultures, etc., nearer each other.

We have had the Aryans and the Dravidians, the Hindus and the Buddhists, the Muslims and the Christians, the Jews and the Zoroas-trians. Today we are facing another challenge, the challenge of modernism, new ideas, industrial progress and other things, and we should preserve the essential values of our culture. So the process of national integration that we talk of is a perpetual process. It is never finished. It is always going on and we must try to bring about national unity and national integration. These are the ideals which we should aim at.

The Sanskrit heritage constitutes the basis, so to say, of almost all our culture, of all our literatures, and that starts with the emphasis on the dignity of man, the potential divinity of the individual. The four Vedas themselves have their *mabavakyas* or the great saying which assert the potential divinity of every individual. These sayings from the four Vedas tell us that we should try to find out what constitutes the real nature of the human individual. So a reflective temper has been induced in us, so as to realize the potential divinity that we have. Even from images which we come across in the Mohenjodaro culture, we find one in rapt meditation, with closed eyes and indrawn, trying to find out what the truth of things is.

Apart from this democratic basis, the next thing is in the creative silence of each individual. He is to find out what the truth happens to be. Later on, in the middle ages when different languages came up, we tried to adapt the ancient culture into different versions. You have the *Ramayana* translated into Tamil by Kamban, and by Ranganatha and Bhaskara in Telugu. You have *Ramacharit Manas.* But one essential thing is: there must be continuity preserved. *Nana purana niga-magama sammatam.* In other words, when Tulasidasa is writing his *Ramacharit Manas* he emphasises them, trying to be in conformity with what has ben asserted in the different *puranas, nigamas and agamas.* He is not trying to run away into a different track altogether, but he is trying to be more or less acceptable to these different things. *Sammatam* is the word used. It must be acceptable to it. So even though creative writers have produced wonderful works, expressing their own creativity in different languages, there has been the common background which they are trying to assert, which they are trying to establish through their own works.

Another feature which has come down to us is what is now called secularism, what has been called a kind of hospitality to every kind of faith. The *Rg Veda* says, *ekam sad vipra bahudha vadanti*. The *Bhagavadgita* says:

ye yatha mam prapadyante

tarns tathai 'va bhajamy aham

mama vartma 'nuvartante

manusyah partha sarvasah

We are still asserting what may be regarded as that understanding acceptance of variety of forms of beliefs and converging purpose, in the historic task assigned to this country, of bringing together a variety of cultures, races, religions, etc.

We should not think this task is over. It is still ahead of us. We have not been able completely to integrate the different faiths and the different cultures here. We must try to work out these objectives on the principles which have come down to us, democracy, secularism and the abolition of the differences between the rich and the poor, as far as possible. Complete elimination is not possible. So this task of national unity, national integration, is something which awaits us still and we are called upon to work for it through our literary media, through the plays we write, through the stories we bring out.

Through all these things we are called upon to carry out the different things, integrate them and present a picture of one India. Unity, democratic basis, acceptance of all the cultures and all the faiths in an understanding way, these are the main principles which have come down to us from four to five thousand years and it is these principles which we have to lay our hands on and try to use them in the production of any literary works.

Languages like Urdu, to which we have not paid adequate attention, and Sindhi also, many people in our country use them, these languages will also have to be utilised. Of the languages we have in our Schedule, some are Sanskritic and some are Dravidian, but there is interaction between them. That has happened because there has been this correlation of our cultures, integration of different sides of our life. These have been going on for centuries, yet unfinished. If there is any lesson which this country has for the world, it is just this; India happens to be the laboratory where different cultures, different religions, different races, have met together and if we are able to succeed in the task of integrating them all, the world platform, which has also got a variety of communities, races and religions, may be able to succeed in the endeavour of building up a world community while preserving variety.

Diversity is the essential aspect of any community. And if it is so, while preserving the diversity, it will be possible for us to develop a kind of single community. The production of such a world community is the task assigned to this particular generation and what we achieve in our country may be of help to the world at large.

FRUITS OF KNOWLEDGE

The one fact of our age is the confrontation of different cultures and different religions. Once upon a time we used to have religions working in parallel lines without much influence on one another. Today we are thrown together. The world has become a physical unity. There is nearness and neighbourhood. But it should also become an integrated entity.

How have religions been functioning? When you emphasize the formal aspects of religions, they divide the world. When you emphasize the inner, the deeper spiritual side of religion, they unite the world. We must try to find out what the real significance of religion is. The religious quest is not something which is supererogatory. Every human individual has the craving to find out what this world consists of. Is this cosmic panorama all? Or is there a constant presence behind, informing, animating and giving life to this whole cosmic process? It is the question which we raise. Every thoughtful person has raised it. The *Gita* says, *anityam asukham lokam.* The *Upanisad* writer tells us: this world is *asat,* unreal; this world is *mrtyu,* death; this world is *tamas,* darkness. Is there a way out? That is the question which he asks.

The Buddha, when he saw the signs of old age, sickness and death, asked, 'Is this all, or is there anything we can get from out of this succession of mundane states?' He met a yogi who said: Oh! best of men! Afraid of this life of birth and death, I have given up this world. For what? For liberating myself from this circuit of *samsara.* I am struggling to find whether there is anything eternal, anything which breathes on the temporal or whether these succession of stages leading to annihilation are all. But simply because we ask for something, it does not follow that, that something has a reality. I may ask for food but food may not be there.

You may ask whether there is anything which exists behind the panorama; but simply because you ask for it does not follow that it is there. So we try, as reasonable beings, to find out by reason, by logical reflection — whether there is anything. The answer we give is, 'Try, look at the world, look at the experience, look at how things happen.' From matter we go to life; from life we go to *manas,* mind; from *manas* we go to *jnana*, intelligence; from intelligence we rise to *ananda*, Absolute Reality, freedom. The cosmic process is a staircase, so to say, leading from one stage to another.

By means of logical reflection we assert that there is some reality, something which serves as the basis of all. But intellectual speculation is different from spiritual realization. We cannot be satisfied with logical inference. There is a difference between saying, 'There is God', and feeling the reality of God in our nature; *anubhavavasanameva vidya phalam.* The fruit of knowledge, the fruit of *vidya* is *anubhava.* So we say no man can be regarded as truly fulfilled unless he is able to rise from the discords, doubts and difficulties of intellect and gets himself illumined, rises to a higher state of consciousness; when he gets pure tranquillity of spirit; when he is able to say, 'I have known the truth.'

If, therefore, we raise the question whether there is anything, we infer logically that there should be something, and we see face to face. This seeing face to face requires a churning of our mind, a discipline of our whole being. We must be transformed in our nature. We must be different from what we are. That is the meaning of attaining *anubhava* or illumination. It is the man who has so changed himself that he can say he has seen the Reality — not others. 'Blessed are the pure in heart for they shall see God.' Seeing of God is a consequence of purity of heart. We must change ourselves so completely that we can say, ‘I have seen the Supreme. In my lifetime, in my flesh, I have seen the Ultimate Reality.’

But people with *anubhava* have given different accounts of Reality. Which are we to accept? Kanada says one thing, Jaimini says another thing. What is it that we have to take for granted? Our scriptures have been emphatic, from the beginning, that there must be hospitality so far as the treatment of the Supreme and of the prayers we address to Him are concerned. If we are able to say that, then we will see that the descriptions which are given — halting, imperfect as they are — they ought not to be made to conflict with each other. There is a harmony, *samanvaya* reconciliation’ of all these things. We call him Siva, we call him Visnu, we call him the Buddha, we call him by any name; but the metaphysical reality is one and the same.

We know the verse which says: I am a Saivite.

I chant the *pancaksart mantra Corn namab sivaya)* but my heart turns to the darling of the Gopis.

janardano va mahesvaro va

na vastu-bhede-pratipattir asti

Whether you call it *Janardana* or *Mahesvara*, there is no distinction in reality. These are names, but all roads lead to the same God, the same Supreme, and we should not quarrel about names we give to it.

The question, the logical answer, the intuitive illumination and a spirit of harmony among the descriptions, etc., which we have, this is nothing dogmatic, nothing sectarian, nothing peculiar to this or that; it is something which has come down to us from the beginning of our history. We find there: *tad visnoh paramam padam sada pasyanti surayab. Pasyanti* is the word used. We see the divine nature, where it dwells and then the way in which we describe it:

esa devo visvakarma mahatma

soda jananam hrdave sannivistah

hrda manisa manasabhiklipto

ya enam viduramrtas te bhavanti

Through understanding, will and imagination, we fabricate that reality into the idiom which suits us. So it will have different forms. It will not have this particular form or that. *Samkaracarya* tells us: *sa ca bhaguvan jnanaisvarya saktibalavirya tejobhih, soda sampannah, trigunatmikam vaisnavim svam mayam mulaprakrtim vasikrtya, ajo avyayo bhutanam isvaro nityasuddhabuddhamnkta-svabhav' opi san svamayaya debavan ivajata iva, lokanugraham kurvanniva laksyate.* That one Supreme assumes different forms to oblige suffering humanity.

He comes in the form of the Buddha, Mahavira, Nanak, or any of the great teachers. They are all messengers of the Supreme Light and the messengers may not always agree with one another but the harmony of all descriptions is the essential fact of our religion. So far as these spiritual aspects are concerned, so far as these personal expertences are concerned, we listen to what people have to say, *sravana;* we think about what they say, *manana;* we make it part of our being, it becomes *atma darsana.* It is equated with the insight into the Supreme itself.

Similarly, the *Gita* tells us *tad viddhi pranipatena pariprasnena sevaya. Pranipata* is listening to a teacher, prostrating ourselves; *pariprasna* is cross-examining him, asking him all questions. *Seva,* by service to Him we assimilate the truth, make it a part of our very being. We become different. Human fulfilment is the answer to man's question. He is not really a realised soul if he merely repeats texts, discusses philosophy. It is a prophetic soul, it is the man who has experienced it, who is the true individual. Priestly religion in one thing; the philosophical religion is another; the prophetic religion is the highest. It is there that the individual himself becomes a messenger of Light.

While these things are accepted through

out the world as forming the basic background of India's thought, we have not adhered to it systematically. We have diverted ourselves, we have gone away from the true path. We think by doing this or doing that we are likely to attain salvation. That is a wrong thing. About the caste system, for example, *Vedanta Desika* says:

> *syapaco'pi mahipala visnubhakto dvija-dhikah*
>
> *visnu bhaktr vihinasca yatis ca svapa-cadhamah*

If we do not have that spirit in us, if we have not got love of God, if we have not got the sense of spiritual values; it is not a question whether we are born this way or that way; even if we are dog-eaters, if we have got love of God, we are the highest of all; if we do not have it; then we are lower than the lowest. In other words, that caste we belong to, to what condition we belong, is a matter of our character, the way in which we behave

vrksan chitva pasun hatva krtva rudhira-kardamam

yady evam gamyate svargam narakam kena gamyate

If by cuiting trees, killing animals, making blood flow, we attain salvation, what is the way to hell, the critic asks. In other words, we are doing things which are exactly opposed to the fundamental preachings of our religion. We do them and if our people are condemned and criticized, if they do not get on well in other countries, it is because they are not the representatives of the spiritual culture of our country. They are the representatives of the traditional dogmas and usages.

Let us understand in what the essence of our culture consists, what is Hindu *Dharma*, and that we should not practise things which are really opposed to Hindu *Dharma*. Every day we do them. We believe in God, but do things which betray our adherence to the world, the flesh and the devil. Anyone who believes in God will not adopt attitudes which we sometimes adopt. We have to scrutinize ourselves, examine ourselves, ask ourselves every day a question, whether we are truly believers in God or merely counterfeit believers. That is what we have to understand.

I do hope that if our religion rids itself of these pernicious practices which in the growth of centuries have come about, it will be able to consolidate this world, it will be able to tell people that there is a religion which has allowed peaceful friendly co-operation among all. Whether it is the Hindu, the Buddhist or Sikh or Jain or other religion, it does not look down on anybody. So long as we have belief in God and adhere to certain spiritual values, we will always be regarded as truly religious men. If we do not have it, however much we may talk, however much we may read scriptures, we will not be considered truly religious men.

Our religion has moved from stage to stage — we had the *Vedas*, then we had the *Upanisads*, then we had the *Gita;* then we had the *Acharyas.* the *Bhaktas,* and today also we have people who belong to the real core of our religion. There are representatives of the true spirit of religion. We may not recognize them; but there are quite humble, unostentatious souls who are perpetually changing themselves, perpetually meditating, all the time trying to find out what is wrong with them and what they should do to make themselves worthy of the great traditions of our culture.

Creed Of Wisdom And Love

Every society has a soul as well as a body. These things help to make our bodies strong and at the same time we must do something to enrich our spirit if we are to sustain ourselves properly in this country or in the world. Both these aspects, the spiritual and the physical, constitute the nature of any society.

You find two sides in the Buddha's life, meditation, leading to the development of enlightenment, and service of humanity the rest of the time. These two, enlightenment and service, constitute the essentials of any religion. At the time of the Buddha, though there were teachers in our country who said that *atma jnana* or knowledge of the self is essential, more important than the mere performing of ceremony, etc., most of the humanity in this country were practising the rituals. Without the knowledge of the Reality which is enlightenment in our own nature, by doing outward rituals we do not understand the real significance of religion.

A man will have to think within himself, concentrate his attention and try to realise what is the Reality which is there, of which all these things are the expression. The Buddha was dissatisfied with the way in which religion was practised in those days and said, as another prophet says, 'We want mercy, not sacrifice'. We want real help, love of humanity. That is what we require and we do not require all other formulae and ritualistic ceremonies. He condemned rituals and made out that diese rituals do not take us to the Ultimate Truth. If we want to attain the Truth, we will have to do exacdy what the Buddha did.

He looked at the world, met the sights of a

sick man, an old man, and a dead man. Death, old age, sickness, are the perils to which human flesh is exposed. Is therc any way to get out of these things? He then met a sàdhu, a monk, who was looking bright. He asked him, 'How is it, in this world so full of sorrow, that you are able to have an appearance of brightness?' The monk simply said: O, best of men, afraid of birth and death, I have become a monk, a wanderer, without any settled abode, to escape from the tyranny of Time.

Time has for its symbol birth and death, and if you wish to overcome time, if you wish really to obtain *nirvana,* that is merely escape from time; not escape from the time in the sense that we avoid temporal things but escape from subjection to time. *Nirvana* is not only time-transcending, it is also time-transforming. After we attain enlightenment, we indulge in the affairs of the world by trying to transform, though we try to redeem time and make it eternity. It is not life in time with the proper perspective in our mind. That has been the gospel which the Buddha taught: escape from time and at the same time control over time. That is the way in which we have to live in this world and the rest of time we have to devote ourselves to the service of humanity.

His whole life is a succession of these two sides. Trying by every possible means to attain enlightenment; and once he became enlightened, he spent himself in the service of humanity. These two things, wisdom and love, they constitute the essence of every religion and the Buddha emphasised those two things in his life, gave us practical illustration that we have to live in this world to acquire wisdom and to spend our life in the service of humanity. That is what he attempted to do. So if you wish to know what constitutes the real essence of religion it is illustrated by the life of the Buddha. His own career is there.

Unfortunately, so many other things have

also come up and so many sects arose even in Buddhism. It became a scholastic, dogmatic and sectarian religion. We have to get back to the original purity, vigour and dynamism, all that the Buddha stood for. Each man must descend into the depth of his consciousness and discover there a permanent religion of which everything else is the expression; and once he has attained that kind of wisdom, he must be serving humanity.

Wisdom and love, these are the two things which should be regarded as constituting the essential aspects of the Buddha's religion. He said that life is suffering and suffering has a cause and we can escape from suffering and we can attain *nirvana* or enlightenment. It is not something which is beyond our scope. It is possible for us to attain *nirvana* here and now. It is not essential for us to escape into another world. If we wish to become truly enlightened here and now by constant practice or deep meditation, it will be possible for us to attain enlightenment.

When once we have that enlightenment, then we go out into the world; we do not withdraw from the world but we participate in it. We get involved in it; all the time we are working for the uplift of humanity. If this temple suggests to us, inspires us with these ideals of self-knowledge and love of humanity it will have done a useful service. It is for that that we go to a temple.

There is a verse which tells us that the right kind of religion is soaking yourself in the spirit of the Divine, in the spirit of the spiritual; the second way is by contemplation and meditation; if even that is not possible for you to do, you take to image worship; and if even that is not possible you do *homa* and *yatra:*

uttama sahaja vastha dvitiya dhyanadharana

tritiya pmtimapuja homayatra caturthika

The man who is possessed by God, who is a truly emancipated being, who is really divine, is one who lives constantly in the spirit of God, naturalises in the atmosphere of God; and not those who put on costumes and tell us they are the teachers.

A truly religious man has to perform things which cost him a lot, as the Buddha did; he gave up his palace, his kingdom, his wife, his child, because religious life is something that costs us enormously. It is not something which we can purchase from a grocery shop or a drug store. It is something which we can get by passing through stern discipline, by going through a travail of spirit. Most of us practise religion, go to temples, churches, etc., think that we are religious, but in our hearts all the time there are irreligious things. So, what is necessary is a process of establishing victory over the impediments to the insight into the Ultimate Reality. Achieve it by intellectual and spiritual struggle; you will be a different man and your works will have a greater value than what you are able to possess.

Man Has Yet To Grow

Humanity sometimes feels orphaned. Is there a God? Why are we in this unfortunate position? Why are people crucifying one another? That is a kind of curse. In such circumstances, Sadhu Vaswani gave us hope and said, 'Beyond the clouds, the Sun still shines.' Beyond the *tamas* or the darkness, there is the brilliant sun-coloured deity. Don't lose heart simply because you happen to be in distress or disappointment. That was the message which our ancient *Upanisads* gave us.

That great Supreme Light, again and again, sends to this world, which is in the midst of darkness, delusion, etc., His messengers to lift up the people and to waken them up. The messengers of Light are the *avataras,* the gods, the prophets whom we worship.

If this country lives in spite of all the troubles it has passed through, if it is going to survive, it is because it believes that it is not by mere security and survival that we live, but by the plenitude of the human spirit which will assert itself on every side of our nature, that the divine conscience will permeate all the affairs of the world, and every human being will himself grow into his higher nature.

Man is something to be surpassed, man is not the end of evolution, man has yet to grow — it is that feeling that we have. We, as human beings, are full of discords and difficulties. We are much bigger than minerals, plants, animals. We are human beings; but the human being is not the end of it all. The human being has to become something superhuman. He has to become, realize the spark which is there in his nature. We do not realize that it is there, infusing energy and wealth of spirit into all our activity.

It is the forgetfulness of the Divine which is in us, which is responsible for so much distress and disappointment which you have in this world. The work of man is to grow into something higher than himself. This world consists of minerals, plants, animals, human beings, God-possessed souls. We have to become God possessed souls; we have to rise from our present state of imperfection, ignorance, to a state of tranquillity of spirit and equanimity of mind where we look upon all human beings as our kindred, as members of one family. It is that which is the goal set to human beings.

Women, after all, are much nearer to the roots of Reality than men. I used to quote the verse which was written in Tirupati by a young girl from Kerala who went there and said :

ratnaikaras tava grham jaya ca laksmi
kirn deyam asti bhavate purusotamaya
abhiragopa-lalana hriamanasaya
dattam mano me tvaritam grhana

Your home is *Ratnakara..* You are wedded to prosperity. What is it I can offer to you, *Purusottama, Manasakitiman?* What is there that I have to offer to you? You have got *Ratnakara* as your abode, Laksmi is your wedded wife and I offer you my heart, take it quickly, do not hesitate about it, for Heaven's sake.

That kind of complete surrender, complete prostration, complete faith in the Divine was there in Mira's life. That is what Mira stands for. Troubled as she was, tabulated as she was, put to so much of discomfort and inconvenience as she was, she never deserted her faith in the Supreme. It is that alone that can save this country and that is saving it.

We are not yet deserted by God. He has not given up as hopeless. Therefore, it is possible for us to think that there is some Divine force in this world, producing, stage after stage, unfolding, different values of this world. That is why we are here. We are called upon to come into this feast of life, so that we might grow bigger, mightier than we happen to be.

Never despair! There is no malice in circumstances. It will be possible for us to overcome all the obstacles that come and threaten us and we will be able to rise higher than we are. This world is bound to become a fit habitation for humanity, whatever the circumstances today may make us feel. Anybody who has faith in the Divine will feel that there is no such thing as determinism, mechanical, logical or historical, as there is God who puts hope and understanding. We can overthrow all these things and bring about a better universe than what we have.

The Challenge Of Life

We put on a sacred thread and call ourselves *vipras* or learned people. We put on the orange robes and call ourselves *sanyasins*. It is not the thread, it is not the clothes, that make a man learned or a monk. These are external symbols intended to develop in us the true attitude of learning and renunciation. If you do not have them, you are not a learned man, you are not a renouncer.

The trouble in our country — it has been so for a long time past — is that we have had religion in plenty for centuries. What have we done with that religion? Do we regard one another as members of one common family? Do we regard all our people as belonging to one central fellowship?

Do we look upon their sufferings as our own and their enjoyment as our own? So long as that is not there, our religion is a sham, it is a facade and it is something to be discarded and not to be adopted with any seriousness.

If you call yourself a truly religious man you must develop that spirit of renunciation and that spirit of social service which has marked the greatest saints and sages of our country. For one saint or sage you have a hundred frauds who pose to be saints or sages. I want you to beware of all these frauds and get away from their path and make them feel what they are. Deep religion is the true spirit of humility, renunciation and service. That is what I meant when I said we have enough religion to hate one another but not enough religion to love one another!

A library has a central place in any centre of learning. It has been so from time immemorial. We have had libraries in our country, though not in such imposing buildings. Our great teachers, our pandits, etc., had their libraries in their memories; some of them on palm-leaf manuscripts; others, after printing came, in collections of books. It is necessary for each one of us to develop a library of his own, to have a select set of books, books which interest him, enchant him, to which he can turn whenever he is in distress or which he can enjoy if he whishes to do so.

A book is different from other media of communication. It requires you to be alone, it requires you to be silent. It requires you to sit with concentrated attention on the book which you are reading. Nowadays it is easier to write books than to read them! Some of us have written books and we know how difficult it is to read those books now! In other words, you must develop the quality of silent meditation if you want to absorb the contents of any particular book.

The great books of the world belong to all countries and all ages. They have a universal quality about them. A distinguished Master of Balliol when he was called upon to mention three books which he would carry with him in his onward journey, if he were told that he would have no other books given to him, mentioned, being a Christian, the Holy Bible, Shakespeare and Kant's Critique of Pure Reason. These are the three books which he mentioned.

These books are well known in our country. Here we would say, our religious books, our Kalidasa, and our philosophers. These are the people who educate us, who are responsible for making our minds sensitive, making them responsive to every kind of human situation. If Kalidasa and Shakepeare are universal in their nature it is because they respond to the variety of human nature. They speak to us not only of the tumult of the human soul but of the depth of the human soul, the poetry, the pathos, the beauty and compassion through which every human being passes.

These passions are common to human beings wherever they happen to be, whether they are

Indians or Englishmen, American or Japanese; whoever opens a book like that experiences all that and finds himself face to facc with the true nature of humanity. That is why the greatest artists are regarded as universal in their character. It is so with regard to scientific books; it is so with regard to literary works; it is so with regard to masterpieces of art; it is so with regard to great compositions of music. You will find they have a touch of the universal. They lift you out of your particular climate, they make you breathe the air of universality, they make you feel whether you come from the East or from the West you are the same human being. At a time like this when the East and the West are getting nearer, when you are trying to establish not merely the United Nations which is a political organisation but that which symbolizes the human family, the family of nations, it is necessary for us to develop a taste for these great universal works, whether they come from England or America, India or Japan, it does not matter. It is that kind of taste that we have to cultivate and create.

One of our popular verses tells us: *samsara visa vrksa.* In this poisoned tree of *samsara,* if you wish to have a few glimpses of eternity, if you want to escape from what is fugitive and fragile, if you want to touch an element of beatitude, if you wish to feel that you are not of the earth earthy, you must read classical works and you must commune with great minds. You must be able to absorb the essence, the quintessence, so to say, of great works. Every great book is the distillation of your perfect experience. It is the product of the deepest moments of your insight. You merely pour out your soul into it. If you want to know the nature of a particular writer, you need not ask him what he did and what he had passed through. You have merely to open here and there the book or his writing and find out the company he keeps and what sort of man he is A man's essence comes out in his expressions, most characteristically in his literary expressions.

Depth Of Life

Wheiher it is literature proper or phi-losophy or history, you can always use the enchanted word which conveys not merely understanding but inspiration. We have had many great philosophers in the world — Plato, Locke: in our own country *Samkara.* They are men who used language to its perfection. They were able to convey what they intended to convey unlike some who use violence of phrase and poverty of thought, not by those things but by dignity of diction and depth of experience.

A great creative writer must have a vision which he is attempting to translate into words. He must have the richness and the depth of life and experience. Unless we ourselves pass through these, it will not be possible for us to convey our own depth to other people. So it is not a question of mere literary equipment and superficiality of thought, but you must dive into the depths of life. You must try to discover the secret which is there, the secret which expresses itself and the magic and majesty of the comic panorama, natural and historical.

While the whole world is changing, some of us resist change in this world even today. It will not be possible to do the impossible. When the whole thing is a movement, and we call it *samsara*, that which perpetually flows and does not top at any time, how can we resist change? How can we bring about a static India in the midst of a changing world? It is for the creative writers, whatever may be their subject, to bring about a change and educate the people of our country to acc-ept change as something which is natural and desirable In this country we suffer not so much from external threats as from dangers within.

We will be able to resist any kind of external threat if we are strong, if we are united, if we are progressive. If we are unablc to achieve these qualities and integrate our whole country into a real whole, not merely a superficial whole of existing within a particular geographical area, but if we are able to develop an organic union of minds and hearts among the people of our country, it will be possible for us to resist any kind of outer threat. Nations perish not from external threats but from their inward decay. It is that which we should resist and I hope the creative writers will take it into their minds and hearts that they have a great reponsibility to fulfil in this changing world.

I hear now and then of decline of compassion, the death of the human heart, that men have become merely automata, robots. They do what the other man does; they do not think for themselves. There is nothing spontaneous about them, creative spontaneity is killed in them;

they become duplicates of one another. I do not think this criticism is correct. There is so much social passion today, so much compassion, when people go about saying, 'Why are we subjecting millions of our people to cast restrictions and other things? Why are we fighting on religious issues, on racial issues, on linguistic issues, etc.?'

It is therefore not true to say that compassion has declined, that social passion has declined. We have to take into account these qualities and apply them to the removal of the restrictions and disabilities from which many of our people suffer today. Individually we are compassionate and courageous. When we act as members of groups, we lose these human qualities and become merely ants in an anthill or follow the herd instinct. A sense of compassion for others is the one quality which lifts humanity above the level of brutes.

We have a story in the *Bhagavata* which speaks

to us of Draupadi. Draupadi's five children, the *upapandavas,* were killed by *Asvatthama* and Arjuna comes and says, 'Dear Draupadi, I will bring *Asvatthama's* head to you on a platter.' What is the answer which Draupadi gave?

ma rodid asyajanani gautami patidevata yatha
aham mrtavatsa arta rodimya-srumukhi muhuh

'Let not Gautami, the mother of *Asvatthama,* weep like me with my children dead before me. Why should she also suffer a similar fate to mine? Arjuna, don't touch *Asvatthama.* Leave him alone.'

There you have the heart of India speaking. Even though her children were killed by *Asvatthama,* the mother of those children tells Arjuna, 'Don't hurt *Asvatthama,* let not his mother, *asya janani Gautami patidevata* weep as I am weeping here today.'

There are several things in our epics which we may profitably use. There are many other things which we have to discard. But this quality of compassion is the voice of true humanity. It is that which we need most today, both in our country and in the world.

That is the natural bond. All these restrictions of caste, community, race and religion are artificial. They are contingent. They are not the essence of humanity. They do not belong to the greatness of human nature. They belong to the artificial restrictions that have been imposed on us by accidents of geography and history. We should not make them the fundamental aspects of humanity.

Our Common Heritage

Many of our people do not know the first principle of what the Indian heritage is. They have no conception of what the general outlook of our country is. It is something which is held up by the application of a scientific method to the mastery of the ultimate problem of thought and life.

In one of the *Upanisads*, it is said, "I want to learn 'Brahma'." The answer is, *tapasa. Brahma vijinasasva-tapo Brahma. Tapas* is not merely performing austerity. *Tapa alocane.* It is the reflection, reflection on the world which we see outside. When we look at the world outside we find that it can be accounted for in many different ways. Philosophy is a criticism of categories. You start with lower inadequate ones and progress gradually to the highest category.

In that *Upanisad,* matter, life, mind, intelligence and spirit are given in an ascending scale. Spirit is the principle which accounts for the whole universe. Intelligence cannot account for it, mind cannot, life cannot, matter cannot; they can account for certain segments of this life, but the only ultimate comprehensive principle, which can account for the whole universe, is spirit. This comes from an objective examination of the universe.

It is also possible to undertake a subjective survey. You discover there, you live in different state of consciousness. The waking world of *jagrat,* the dream world of *svapna,* the dreamless sleep of *susupti,* and beyond thee three there is an ultimate transcendent consciousness which is called *turiya.* You give it *ekatmat pratyaya saram prapanco-pasamam santam sivam advaitam.* But this cosmic principle and this ultimate principle in man are not different. *Ayam atma brahma* — that *Brahma* is the Supreme Self. Simply because it is not possible for you to account for it in categories of human language or logical proposition, it does not become a mere nullity.

It is *Samkara* who tells us that these things, which are indescribable *digdesaguna phalabheda rahitam paramarthasad advayam brahma mandabuddhinam asad iva pratibhati*, can hardly be discerned by the feeble-minded. This ultimate category, the Ultimate Reality, which transcends all distinction appears to be *asat* but it is really the perfection of Reality, because it is the depth of all realities; so, that is the first principle. Because it is incomprehensible by human language or human categories it does not follow that it is merely an unreality. We must, therefore, be hospitable to every kind of description which men adopt. So it is that hospitality of the mind which accepts every description, every approximation to *atma*, is accepted.

You find here, therefore, an Ultimate Reality which is the supreme self in your own being and which can be expressed in many forms. It has many messengers to carry that light. All these are to be accepted by us, and then if we want to live in this world, we get recognition of that Ultimate Reality. Discipline, austerity, these things are essential. We are called upon, therefore, to practise spiritual exercises to see that light within ourselves; it is the light in us

If we do that we will not have quarrels with others; we will not be cast out without any kind of hope; we will not be haunted by despair; even if things crash it will be posssible for us to assert that there is something in us which is superior to the whole environmental state.

At a time like this when the world has become unstable, when it is precarious, when it is not self-perpetuating, it does not automatically progress, it is necessary for us to recognize the reality of the Ultimate within us which is proved and that through this impetus any progress can possibly be achieved.

It is my earnest hope that this heritage will become the common possession not merely of all Indians but of all people in the world. There is nothing sectarian about it. It is scientific, it is ethical, it is spiritual. We have forgotten it — we have confused it with so many extraneous things that crept within our religion and practice, we have to discard all those things. There are many things in our heritage of which we cannot be proud, but there are many things again which are our pride. Let us cling to the latter and discard the former to ensure our progress on right lines.

Growth Of Knowledge And Wisdom

All cultures have one supreme aim in view, namely, enabling you to know the truth of things — *sawa satra prayojanam atma darsanam.* The motive, the end and ambition of all *sastras* is *atma darsanam,* insight into the Reality, the capacity to find out what the Ultimate Truth of things is That has been the aim of every kind of scientific endeavour, whether it belongs to natural sciences or humanistic studies.

There is a general criticism levelled against us that where our knowledge of nature is increasing our wisdom is diminishing. The spectacular achievements of science are very impressive and they have got such great power in their control that they can devastate the world. If there are people who contemplate the results of nuclear developments they will feel: what is it that has happened to man, why is it that he has increased so much in wordly power, has so much extended his body through his control over radio, television and other machines, and yet his soul seems to be stagnant? It is not growing correspondingly.

There is disproportion between the growth of wisdom and the increase of knowledge. It is that disparity that has impressed many people. Let us try to extend our understanding of the nature of things; let us have certain values which will be utilized by the mechanical devices and contrivances we have brought about. It is necessary for us to know, whatever may be the nature of science, it is the spirit of man that is expressing itself there.

Every human individual must look upon himself not as living on the outer surface of things. There is a living depth in him. There is a centre there which persists, which abides, whatever may be the change. *Vacaspati* tells us: *e su vyavartamanesu yad anuvartate tat lebhyo bhinnam.* That which abides in the revolving world, in the rotating wheel of time, where all things are revolving, there is till a centre in each human being and it is that centre that constitutes the fountain-head of truth and wisdom and enlightens us. If we overlook that centre, if we merely live on the surface of things, if we are dealing with machines and make ourselves into machines, this danger will become really great and we will get alienated from our true spirit.

So it is that whatever be our knowledge, scientific or humanistic, understand it as the expression of the wondrous mind of man, beautiful spirit, which is there, the liquid flame of consciousness. If we look at the surface of things, we overlook the reality which is the supreme source of everything great. We have to see if this side of knowledge is increasing, if wisdom is diminishing.

If that kind of criticism is hurled against us, it

is due to neglect of the spiritual side, due to the neglect of human beings who are concentrating themselves on the externals of life, little realizing that these externals are to be employed for the purpose of promoting human wisdom. So wisdom and knowledge will have to grow together.

Everything in this world has been a means or an instrument for grasping of the Eternal. Even the arts in which we dwell, the arts that we foster, they are said to be *kala-kam paramatmanam lati grhnati iti kala.* That by which we grasp the Eternal, that is said to be an art and its purpose is to refine the spirit of man — *atma samskriti vava silpani.* All sciences are there but we are incapable of using them for refining our own spirit. We have said it so often but in our practice we overlook it.

The whole world has to become our home. The other day I had the opportunity of speaking to His Holiness the Pope. I pointed out to him that when Christianity arose, its spiritual environment was limited to Greece and Rome. The Jewish soul was mixed up with Greek thought and Roman organisation and we have Christian doctrine today. St Thomas Acquinas tried to reconcile Aristotelian thought with Christian theology; he took for granted that Aristotelian thought represented secular disciplines of the world and he wanted to bring them together. Today the whole world has become the spiritual environment of every religion. If it is to exist, if it is not to fade away, if it is to survive, it must come to terms with all the great sciences, with all the great traditions of religious thought. There is a reconciliation, so to say, of Christianity with every religion and of every religion with Christianity. They are all the common heritage of man.

Knowledge Of The Self

If we live today, it is not because of our great industrial progress or mechanical efficiency or our atom bombs and things like that. We live today because there are still people who illustrate for the commonalty the path of spirituality and their behaviour is something which is divinely ordained. It is such people who represent the true culture of our country, *adhyatma vidya:* of all sciences, the greatest science is the knowledge of your own self.

What is the self? Is it flesh and bone, is it muscle and blood, is it merely the mechanical components of your life? Self is something which is beyond all these things. It stands above all these things. *Vacaspati* says, that which is Constant to all your activities, which changes from moment to moment, that is the creative element in one, that is the principle of subjectivity and inward freedom. If you merely become an item in a series of happenings in this world, if you are merely made by nature, you have not got this spirit which asks us to go forward, to develop, so to say. Every man is a dreamer. He dreams for a nobler and better life. He is not merely the victim of the environment in which he is placed. Environment makes the man. Man also makes the environment. He also changes and shapes it. It is that creativity in us which we overlook.

The other day I told an audience that the name Hermitage was given to that beautiful collection of works of art there to indicate to us that man must develop a hermit cell in his own mind and heart if he is to produce great work. No man who merely regards himself a a product of nature can ever bring out a supreme work of art. I am telling you that each man has a solitary and social side to his life. If you are lost in the social side, you will never be able to make history or bring about changes. There is a solitary side. Man must make a monastic cell, sit in judgement and remould that experience and present us a great work of art.

Man is most human when he is lonely, not when he is making speeches, but at a time when he withdraws himself, when he detaches himself from the outer environment and turns within and finds out what it is that is iacking there. Many of us are afraid of looking into ourselves because we have so much there which we do not want to face. We want to avoid it and get away from it. So we become social beings and get away from the realities of our life.

Knowledge of the self is truth, the highest kind of knowledge. That you cannot have by merely looking at the outward environment. You have in the *Upanisad* that great controversy between Narada and Sanatkumara. His pupil says, 'I know every type of *vidya* or knowledge; why is it that I am not able to find that deep solace in my mind? Why is it that I am not able to develop that comfort and peace in my own mind?' He comes to the truth... 'I am only the knower of texts. I have not developed that true knowledge of the self. That is why I am unable to cross the ocean of sorrow.'

Mere textual learning, going to temples, chanting hymns, muttering *mantras,* does not give this spiritual wisdom. You cannot get eternal life by mere textual learning. It will not give you true spiritual wisdom. If you once have that spiritual wisdom, you will be able to perceive the nature of Reality which is above all this phenomenal world and which cannot be expressed in words or in a prepositional form. That is why we have to develop an attitude of hospitality to all other ways of professing religion. That is what our great seers have taught us from the beginning of history And yet today, in the name of caste, of community, we have not been able to develop that national solidarity which is essential for any kind of progress in this world.

You turn to the other countries in the East which have made tremendous progress — Japan. China, etc. What is it you find there? Do people fight there about caste? Do they fight about communal differences? Do they ask what caste one belongs to? These questions are irrelevant. We have to learn this great lesson, that caste differences, communal differences, are all to be put aside and we have to put national welfare and national good as the highest aim of us all. That is what our scriptures have taught us. They have taught us that there is one God and we are all children of that Supreme Light and we should not quarrel about these small things.

We can do so only by self-scrutiny, by having a little time in our life devoted to self-examination, trying to find out whether we have the feelings of egotism, pride, infallibility, a sense of denouncing others and thinking we are the only supreme people. That kind of thing does not make a man a human being. If a man is to deserve the name of humanity, if he is to call himself a truly human being, he must try to rid his mind of all these things — *raga*, *bhaya* and *krodha*.

Freedom Of The Human Spirit

In my own life-time, I have seen so many changes in the world of science — telephones, automobiles, radio, television, aeroplanes, etc. So much of scientific advance is taking place. In the three quarters of this century, work has been done which exceeds the volume of work done in the previous many centuries. It shows how our age is essentially an age of science and technology. In geology also many changes have taken place. Earthquakes, volcanoes, glaciers, wearing away of mountains, disppearance of rivers and change of direction, all of them are of great importance, though these events take long stretches of time to effect themselves. And it is also true that by the study of the rocks and fossils, what is called petrology and palaeontology, some speculation and theories have also been advanced. We are saying that from the unicellular organism through the primate we have come to man. When life arrived, when consciousness comes into being in this world, these are questions which are directly related to investigations which scientists make.

We have a very early *Upanisad* which come from the 8th century B.C. which talks about the cosmic evolution, and it puts down five steps in that cosmic ladder. First of all you have the inorganic, the physical so to say, then you have the biological, pychological, logical, then the mental, then the intellectual and then the spiritual. We have now reached the level of the logical mind, the conceptual mind, which dwells in abstractions, which builds cathedrals, temples, etc., but this is the not the end of human evolution. This logical mind has to grow into the spiritual. The intellectual concept gives us ideas of race, of religion, of nation, which makes us look upon people belonging to other religions and other nations as alien to ourselves,

There are these concepts which are developed by the logical mind of man, what is called *vijnana;* but it is said that this *vijnana* has to grow into *ananda* or the Freedom of the human spirit when it rids itself of shibboleths, when it looks upon the whole world as kindred and makes for common fellowship. That is the idea to which we have to grow. It asserts that man as a logical being is not a final end in human evolution. He is incomplete, imperfect, he has to grow into something higher.

That is coming to us from the scientific side also. The minerals we get, the oils we get, the fuel which we use, these have been the life-line of industrial development. Today we get the uranium also and this uranium is a means by which nuclear weapons can be made. How this nuclear energy is to be used, whether it is for human betterment and progress or for the destruction of fellow human beings and the destruction of all the great arts and achievements which have been built by the hard work and toiling effort of human beings, how it is to happen depends on the spirit of man. This spirit of man has to grow. He has to evolve, he has to take a leap forward.

The human being as he is today, belonging to a particular group limited in its character, if he tries to develop chauvinistic nationalistic concepts, then this uranium which is dug out of the earth's crust may prove to be a disaster to humanity. But if it is to prove of benefit to humanity, it is essential for the human being to grow better. That is where the challenge thrown by the output of uranium on one side and the *upanisadic* concept which tells us that man as an intellectual being is not enough, he is not the final product of evolution, both these things converge. If the challenge of our age is to be met, if this world is to grow into an earthly paradise where human beings can live in freedom, fellowship and friendship, if that is to happen, it is necessary for the human being himself to grow. So it is that we are called upon to use all thc resources available to us for the purpose of perfecting ourselves.

This country, from the beginning of its history, has emphasized another direction of human development. If you look into the Indus Civilization you will find there the image of *mahayogi*, the great ascetic, a man wrapped in contemplation, trying to improve his own nature, trying to establish some kind of conquest over his own passions. You find again in the Buddha, who sits down under the Bodhi tree, trying to lacerate his body and torture his mind in quest of truth. He tells us man has to suffer if he is to grow in his nature. Every kind of quest is related to a conquest; you must be heroic, you must be able to establish your own nature. When Jesus was by the side of the river Jordan, wrapped in prayer and meditation, he was again thinking of the improvement of human nature. So also

Muhammad, when he climbed the mount at Mecca, trying to find out what the truth of things is. He is not outward bound, not looking at the earth, but he is trying to find out how human nature can be developed.

We have so many witnesses of this spirit, you may call it of spiritual discipline, the spirit of holiness. This is the spirit which was exalted by this country for the last fifty centuries, so far as our history goes.

Look at a man like Gandhi. He symbolizes the soul of India, the spirit of India. People came up to him and said, 'You are trying to win freedom for the country but look at history. History tells us no country has ever won its freedom by the methods of truth and love as you suggest.' His answer was, 'Let us not follow the bad example of history. Let us set a good example by trying to achieve national freedom in this country by the methods of non-violence, non-hatred, friendship, *karuna, adroha, maitri*'. These are the ideals which he put before us.

So, from the time of the ancient Indus Valley civilization down to Gandhi and Ramakrishna, you have one spirit, one kind of discipline which they exalted. To make our thoughts conform to spiritual wisdom, to make our will in accordance with the realization of the universal purpose of fellowship, to mould our emotions into harmony with world unity, that is the great cosmic purpose, that is the will of the ages, it is the will of Providence, it is the meaning of history, that we should move forward to fellowship and friendship, to raise ourselves to higher spiritual status. That has been the lesson which this country has adopted and has given to the world also.

Even today we do not exalt military depots or industrial magnates. But a man in a loin-cloth, like Gandhi, or one like Vinoba walking barefoot from place to place, these are the people whom this country exalts. They are the examples to tell us that man in all his scientific glory is nothing comparable to a man who has established supremacy over his own nature. It is the Buddha who said, 'Victory breeds hatred, the conquered live in sorrow.' We should not aim at establishing any kind of material victory. Today, when the world is in a crisis, at a parting of the ways, when we are trying to find out how best we can harness these great nuclear powers, how we can use them for the development of human welfare and not for human destruction, it is the example which this country has put forward which we have to remember.

There are embodiments of holiness and sanctity in every part of the world. Therefore, it is nothing special, it is not the monopoly of this particular country. But we have now to come back to that. We have to realize that man is intended for self-fulfilment, he is not intended for self-destruction. So the great uranium deposits which we are able to get, from which we can make nuclear energy, these things will have to be utilized for the betterment of man, for making this world into a great whole which it is intended to be.

God meant us to love one another and to create. He did not mean us to hate one another and destroy ourselves. That is the parting of the ways. That is the crisis in which we are. And it is essential for the great international scientists who are assembled here to remember something of this spiritual dimension, which this country has exalted from the Indus Valley days down to Mahatma Gandhi. If you are able to do it, you will not only have enriched our material wealth and knoweldge but you will have enriched the resources of humanity, the invisible forces of goodness which are there, latent in every human being, you will be able to bring them out, make them manifest.

It is said there is incarnation. That incarnation is not present in a few individuals. What a few individuals can do, the rest of humanity can also do. We must have the incarnation of the

Supreme in the whole human race. That is what we should attempt to do. Science has given us the facilities necessary. It has brought the world together, it has enabled us to understand the spiritual heritage of every nation, and if we can mobilize the spiritual resources of the whole world, if we are able to put them all into effect, it will be possible for us to make this world a better place than we have found it.

Insight Into Reality

India, during its great days, was never isolated. It was a part of the stream of world history. If you turn to the ancient systems of mathematics or medicine, etc., you will find there the great influence of the Greek, the Roman, the West Asian and other systems. If you turn to the European world you will find that the great advances of science were due to the co-operation of people like Newton, an Englishman, Kepler, a German, Copernicus, a Pole, Galileo, an Italian. All of them collaborated and brought about a scientific revolution of the modern world. So also we were collaborating with the other nations in our great days.

When we fell under subjection, when we

were cut off from the other sources, when we became isolated, our lives became constricted and we were not able to carry the torch that we used to. After political independence was gained, we again came back into the mainstream of history. Our scientists go to different parts of the world and make some small contributions to the advance of the world. They are known today to all parts of the world where science is pursued.

It is necessary that if we want to attack the problems which our country faces — poverty, malnutrition, disease, defective water supply, people dying like flies in some parts of the country — these are all things which must make us feel ashamed of ourselves — it is necessary for us to care for the poor. Attention to the poor is the supreme test by which any government is judged. If we are to be judged to be a civilized society, our first interest must be what we are doing for the thousands of people who are suffering from undreamt of evils — who are the victims, so to say, of all sorts of epidemics and who the like flies on the pavements of our country or in rural areas.

If we want to tackle these problems, it is essential for us to develop science and technology. We must develop these things, we must adopt a scientific outlook. Everyone of us must be endowed with a scientific spirit; obscurantism, superstition and such other things which have weighed us down for centuries must be removed and human beings must feel that they are rational human beings with dignity, with a sense of responsibility, responsibility not merely for what they do but for the poor who are entrusted to their care.

Again and again remarks were made, a special lecture was delivered at Cambridge, saying that a scientific culture and an academic or literary culture are two different things and one has little to do with the other. We produce either seers or technicians; we produce men of intuition, of imagination, or we produce men with mechanical skill, with practical ability, but we do not produce men who are at the same time seers and technicians, people who are able to develop their imagination and at the same time develop their scientific skill. This whole concept of our cultures being divided, of their being two, is something which is, to my mind, unfounded.

Truth is indivisible. Whether it is historic truth, literary truth, or scientific truth, the approaches may be different, but ultimately what we do is exactly the same. It is the imagination that is roused in us by the study of literature, it is imagination again that makes the scientist go forward; his hypothesis makes him remould the environment by which he is presented and makes him bring out the deepest secrets of nature. It is the spirit in man that sits in judgement on the facts of nature, which enables the human being to reshape the environment. We should reshape not merely our outer environment but our inner environment also, our inward forces, the internal power we have, even that has to be remoulded.

The great leaders of countries, the great statesmen have developed astounding power over nature; they have developed spectacular capacity to destroy humanity as well as to save humanity. If we are threatened today by the forces which we have raised, it is not due to forces outside, but lack of control which we have, so to say. It is not weapons that destroy us but it is lack of wisdom. It is the human being who destroys the rest of humanity. If we are to reform ourselves, then science will be the great instrument for the development of the human race, for improving the quality of the human race. That is what we should aim at. All the technical disciplines are there for the purpose of refining the human spirit. *Atma samskrti*, development of human nature, refinement of the human spirit — that is the one supreme aim which we have to put before ourselves.

Most of us think that we are scientists because

we press a button, the light comes up; we press another button, the telephone rings; we press a third button, we get the motor-car outside. But we do not know how these things function. What is the knowledge which is enshrined in these instruments? We know only how to press a button and get something done. That is, we live on the surface of human life — robots, mechanics, technicians. We do not know what the depths of these things indicate and stand for. If we know that, we will never say that science is a different discipline and not human discipline and the other things, literature, history, etc., make a different kind of man. It is not so.

We must study science not from the surface but from its very depth. We must try to understand how all these things happen, how the human being has been able to penetrate into these things and how it has brought about a new transformed world. It is not necessary for us to be technologically or mechanically uniform.

That does not follow. If we have the human spirit cultivated, we will not become mere mechanical robots.

All the branches of discipline have only one end — *sarvasa stra prayojanam atma darsanam.* An insight into Reality is the end of all kinds of discipline. All truth must be regarded as one whole. Whether you practise this discipline or the other discipline, you should practise the one supreme pursuit of truth. It is that which makes a human being dignified and civilized. If you are able to do it, then you become a really civilized human being.

Discipline Of Spirit

We have a Telugu poet telling us that a country does not consist of mere mud, it is the men who have to be rehabilitated.[1] If, today, we are passing through a crisis in our country, it only shows the deterioration that has set in and that deterioration has to be rectified by means of literature, art, painting and sculpture. The investment in spirit is as necessary as the investment in agriculture and industry.

KALA is that which brings us to the realization of the Supreme Spirit; that there is something higher than the passing panorama; that there is some kind of living spirit which animates, informs, inspires all our activities; to make us realize, that is the true purpose of *kala*.

You have literature. Literature should not, or any other art should not, be regarded as merely impressionistic. It is not merely something which you take from outside. If you want to produce great literature, you have to pass through great discipline of spirit. The mind must pass through a travail before it is able to produce any real work of literature or art, whether it is music, dance, drama, sculpture or painting. We cannot merely sit down and take up a paper and scrawl phrases; that is not literature; that is undergraduate literature, the sort of thing in which people generally indulge when they have nothing better to do. You must pass through a travail, through

[1]desamante matti kadoi

desamante manusutoi

complete transformation of your nature. The discipline must change your whole direction of life. It must make you different from what you are and it is only then that you can pour out literature which is of a higher kind.

It is the same with music. You cannot have real music unless the individual is lost in what he plays; he thoroughly enjoys himself when she sings or he sings. That is, you participate in the kind of education you are giving to your audience. You lose your self; you stand out of your self. That is the true meaning of the word ecstasy. Ecstasy means standing out of your own nature. True music lifts you out of your ordinary routine of life, takes you away from the prosaic character of your existence, raises you to a plane of true poetry, true exhilaration, true ecstatic development. It is only then that you have true music.

Similarly with sculpture and painting; it is not merely going about doing something. I was witnessing a painting show in England with Her Majesty the Queen. She was looking at all the things and said, 'Do you know who the author of that painting is?' She said, 'Not a man, but a monkey.' In other words, you attach a brush to the tail and put a canvas and put on the colours. You dip your brush in those colours and you scrawl something and you have a painting of a type; it is not that kind of painting you want.

How did the people of Ajanta caves work? They worked with a spirit of dedication; they were pilgrims of the infinite ; they were people who had no concern for life and light. They were people who devoted themselves to the Supreme Buddha and wanted to bring out in those paintings the best they could from the life of the Buddha. There you have the paintings which will stand for all time. If anything can be regarded as permanent in this world, those paintings will be. So also at Ellora; so also what you find in Mahabalipuram. Did they all work for money? Did they work for recognition? Did they want from this man or that man any kind of pat on their backs? They wrote because they could not help writing; they painted because they could not help painting; they sculptured because there was no alternative to that. It was a necessity imposed on them; it was spiritual necessity. It was because of that that they were able to bring out those mangnificent masterpieces which are today looked upon as wonders of the world.

Here you find a tradition; here you have had many great writers, you have had many musicians, many good dancers, singers, etc. All these were there and you must not believe that dancing is something which is to be regarded as something subordinate; as not worthy of greatly trained human beings. In the *Siva Purana* a description was sought about the *sabha mandapa* and its dimensions. The answer came, A thousand first class women, expert in song and dance and an equal number of men proficient in instrumental music.' The position assigned to men is to play on the accompaniment of instruments, the vital function, or the singing and dancing, these were assigned to women. That is what the *Siva Purana* tells us.

All artists, all poets, whether they belong

to our country or other countries, constitute a brotherhood, so to say. They are the people who knock down the boundaries. When you talk about Mr Churchill, you may have your differences of opinion; but when you talk about Shakespeare, all differences disappear. You stand in admiration of that great genius. So also when you talk of economic or political problems, you may have so many differences; but when you talk about literary, artistic problems, there is a unity of spirit. It is that brotherhood of spirit that is required to be established in a world which is tending to become a mad-house, where people do not understand one another. It is essential for you, therefore, to develop these arts which cross boundaries, which cut across frontiers, and which reveal to us the greatness of the human spirit. It is that that we have to develop.

NOTHING LIKE KNOWLEDGE

There is a motto which says 'Nothing like knowledge'. *Jnana* is not mere information, not mere scholarship, it is not mere criticism, it is education in depth. Whatever subject you take up, you must try to study it, penetrate into it and find out the roots of it. It is not something which is called *pallava grahi panditყam!* It is something which makes you a deep scholar in the subject which you have. *Jnana* without *viveka* is nothing; *na vivekam vina jnanam:* without discrimination, without a sense of right and wrong, if you do not have that sense, if you are not able to accept certain standards in your life and conduct, you may be educated but your life will be degraded and unillumined. If you want to be a true university man, it is essential for us to have certain tenets of conduct, certain forms of behaviour.

It is, therefore, essential that we should try to find out what real education means. It is discrimination, it is the adoption of the right. Everyone has under the surface a streak of violence, a streak which makes him revolt, which makes him rabid, which makes him slay and murder, that streak is there. But you must try to overcome that. The beast in you will have to be overcome if you wish to call yourself a truly educated man. It is there, all the time, pointing out to us that we have a side of our nature which threatens to come out into the open and threatens to make us do things of which we will be ashamed in a cooler hour. You have to put yourself in proper form, so that wisdom may dominate, justice and truth might prevail and not injustice and violence. Democracy and violence do not go together. If you are a true democrat, you may have your differences but you will try to adjust them, you will try to overcome them by mutual settlement. You will never be able to say there is a difference and a difference must always lead to discord and discord must always mean violence. This is not the type of life which you should adopt.

All *sastras* have got only one end in view and that is the insight of the Reality. There are people who believe that science is one thing and humanities another. It is not true. If you find out how a scientist behaves or how a humanist behaves or how an artist behaves, you will find to your satisfaction that all of them have got, more or less, the same *modus operandi.* Do not imagine that the scientists are always observant of facts; they merely accumulate facts. If they think that this world is a comprehensible one, if they think that by accumulating facts you will be able to get some theory, you will discover an element of faith is there Moses was committed to so many difficult things. Suddenly in the burning bush he saw a solution of his problem. The Buddha after great hardship, after a good deal of intellectual endeavour, he came across the tiuth, the truth of enlightenment which enlightened him and the world itself. Archimedes was not able to solve his problem when he was in his study, but when he was in his bathroom he leapt out, saying, 'Eureka', 'I have found out the truth'.

These things come to us not by sheer intellectual endeavour but by the exercise of another which you all possess which enables you to see what the truth of things is. Scientists, too, have emotional intuitions as much as observation and experiment. The humanist also explores, explores the contents of consciousness, explores whatever things are put before him. He has got also the same idea of combination of intuition and understanding, the two go together, may be more in one, may be less in another. But, whether you are a scientist or an artist or a humanist, you will exercise the same resources of your mind — intuitive, intellectual and emotional. You are trying to establish the truth of things, that is what you are attempting to do.

All education is, on the one side, a search for truth; on the other side, it is a pursuit of social betterment. You may discover truth but you should apply it to improve the status of society.

The Majesty Of Law

Law has been ever-growing. It is not a thing which stands still. It is not an end in itself. Take our own Hindu Law: what has happened to the forms of adoption and the types of marriage which we had? They have practically faded out and another kind of law has taken the place of both adoption and marriage laws. This is a thing which happens not merely in law but even in religious forms.

There was a huge controversy in our country once between those who believed in yajna, karma, and etc., those who affirmed the superiority of spiritual wisdom and enlightenment. That controversy was decided by a reference to a lady arbitrator. Mandana Misra was performing a *yajna* when Samkaracharya appeared. *Samkaracharya pada-dvayamm andalastham dadarsa tatah sarvangani viksya samnyasi iti jnatva kopa kolahala cittah kuto mundity ityabravit.* Having seen *Samkaracharya* there in his robes of a *Samnyasin*, Mandana Misra said, Why have you come to disturb the great *yajna* which I am today performing?

When the matter became one of hot controversy and Mandana Misra's wife, *Bharati*, was asked to arbitrate between diese two, I want to tell you how she arbitrated. With purity, detachment, objectivity, dispassion, complete freedom from partisanship with her husband's case, she gave her judgement: 'Of course, spiritual wisdom is superior to mere performance of rites'. That is what *Bharati* said. She gave us an ideal of a good judge, of a good arbitrator. Her relationship with her husband did not count.

The fact that she was to arbitrate between these two great people did not count. Pure objectivity, fidelity to truth, diese were the only things which she had and gave the judgement in favour of Samkaracharya with the result that Mandana Misra became his disciple, became a *Samnyasi, Suresvaracharya,* the first disciple of Samkaracharya, who had his *Mutt* in Sringeri. You see there how things have been moving. You see there also how a woman who was asked to give an award in such a controversy behaved.

We hear nowadays loose talk about 'convicting judges', 'acquitting judges', 'talking judges', 'silent judges', etc. But there is no such thing at all. Bharati merely threw herself into task, studied what the truth was and said, 'This is my judgement. Samkaracharya is right, Mandana Misra is wrong.' This is how she put it. Like that, law is a thing which is prepetually moving, which should respond to the temper, to the traditional patterns as well as the modern tendencies and challenges which face us. All these things will have to be taken into account in judging disputes.

What is the kind of life which we wish to

lead? What does law say? Law has an end in view, the welfare of all people. It is not the welfare of the rich or the well-born but the welfare of every citizen of this country. That is what law aims at and tries to fulfil.

I am reminded of a verse which says, 'Do not talk to me about ancient glories. Let me know what you are at present doing.' It is not necessary for us to take pride in our past. There is a Negro spiritual which says about Jesus's death, "Were you there when they crucified my Lord? Were you there when they laid him in the tomb?" I was at Salt Lake City when this hymn was sung and the head of the Mormon Church there asked me to say a few words. I said, "Why are you raising these hypothetical questions whether you were there two thousand years ago or not? The problem is, what are you doing today? You are crucifying the Lord today, at the altar of racial bigotry, national egotism, etc. What is the fun of merely talking about what happened two thousand years ago?" That is what I remember to have said.

So we must make our courts and institutions proper arbiters of the relations between man and man, between the citizen and the State. If there is to be an end, a goal for our law, that end has been beautifully described in the preamble to our Constitution: Justice, Liberty, Equality, Fraternity. Justice not to be put chased, not to be got by hook or by crook, but impartial justice given to us by people who are wedded to justice and who will interpret the law so that justice may be there. Justice should be immanent in every kind of law, otherwise it is not true justice. A kind of law which voices the will of the strong prevailed long long ago. That is noi law. Justice must cater to the needs of all the individuals, of the citizens and it must be able to give proper judgement on controversies between citizen and citizen, between citizen and State, the States and the Union itself. That is the kind of justice which we have to bring about.

Liberty is a famous concept. No two people are alike: one prefers rubies, another prefers diamonds, a third prefers pearls. We must tolerate. Any society which tolerates differences is capable of defending itself. Any society which puts down difference — nobody can save such an institution. It becomes fanatic and fascist in its character. When we say that so far as forms of religion are concerned we tolerate everything it must not be merely a kind of negative toleration; but it must be a positive appreciation of the values which different religions contain in themselves. We have got it. Whatever name we may adopt, whatever form of prayer we may say, if it is earnestly intended, sincerely felt, it reaches the Ultimate Supreme; and that is what liberty truly means.

Liberty does not mean licence. It is not merely the assertion of rights and the denial of obligations as our friend, the Governor, has just put it to you. You must know not merely the rights but the obligations also which you have. If you overlook the obligations your liberty becomes merely licence. Therefore it is we want this kind of liberty to bc safeguarded in this country. Liberty must be preserved for everyone. Whatever he may do, so long as it is not repugnant to the moral sense of the community and to the general welfare of the people, so long as it is there, liberty will have to be preserved by us.

Equality is a concept which is coming up now. People who have vested interest will always protest against any tendency to equalize. Others will say, 'Why, why should everybody not have the same privileges? Why should not the law protect every citizen?' The law which is administered to every citizen must not be superior to the law which we administer to the highest in the land. The same kind of law must respect both. Law should not be a respecter of persons. It must take every individual for what he is worth. As the seed, so to say, of the political. spiritual and moral authority, it is the individual who must be regarded as the supreme end and not the society or the State. The real point of equality is that the conditions of life must be such that it will be possible for every individual to develop his own character, his own talents. All these things we must be capable of developing otherwise our 'equality' is merely inequality.

There are others who say, 'Inequality is the law of nature. We cannot equalize all people. They are born with different talents and different aptitudes.' But what 'equality' says is that the law must provide equal opportunities. It does not say that we must make all into one. What it says is that the law should provide equal opportunities for all.

When we have 'fraternity', fellow-feeling, we should not only have people belonging to different castes, different communities, etc., but have that basic feeling of charity which binds all individuals together. The development of that feeling, that is the co-operative spirit which we are called upon to undertake. It is not easy for us to judge our own national conduct or ethical standards. We always say a nation has no ethos. It has only interests. We can only judge our nation by the way in which a particular course of conduct subserves its interest or does not subserve its interest. But that kind of idea must be given up. We must bring any kind of settlement of peace under the rule of law.

All nations must be subjected to this criterion of law. What we try to bring about within our own country we should try to bring about throughout the world. That is what we are aiming at. Fraternity means that kind of co-operative union of nations will preserve their variety, their individuality, their distinctiveness, and yet serve the interest of the whole. It is that kind of fraternity we are insisting on. These obligations that we should have are enunciated in the preamble to our Constitution. It is the concept of a good life; the good life is a just life, is a life which tolerates differences, is a life where everybody has got a chance of growing to his highest stature. It is a life where we look upon our own nation as one among many nations, as one which has to serve the community of nations.

These are the ideals that have been set down in our Constitution and people talk about it, speak about it, read about it. It is that Constitution with all its implications of the four conditions given in the preamble. It is that which people should understand and practise to the best of their ability in their daily life. If we do that we will be good citizens of this land. If people lose respect for law and respect for the courts which administer law, it will be a bad day for us. It is essential for the country to respect law, for the Government of the country to respect law and for the courts to maintain the sanctity and purity of legal administration and dispensation of justice. That is absolutely necessary if the rule of law has to be continued in this country as it has to be continued.

Anybody who violates law must be punished. That is the meaning of Civil Disobedience which Gandhiji started, He violated laws but submitted himself to the penalties which law imposed on him. He never tried to escape from those penalties. That is what we should do. If that happens, if our people develop respect for law and if our courts administer law without ill-will, malice, prejudice or favour, there will be growth in the tendency to respect law.

Challenge Of Creative Cinema

Films are the most powerful instrument which we have today so far as mass communication is concerned. They have the widest popular appeal. They engage our whole being — eyes, ears, mind and heart. Millions of people go to films and are influenced by them consciously or unconsciously. They reveal to us the way in which a nation's story has been moulded. They show to us the way in which one nation can speak to another nation.

Films have a universal appeal so long as they have a universal type of human nature or human life for their theme. So far as the basic factors of human experience are concerned, they are the same and are not to be superseded by racial, religious or credal differences. Basically human nature is one. It has the same passions and suffers the same experiences and enjoys the same ecstasies and exaltations. We have the same appreciation and admiration of beauty, the same loathing and contempt for ugliness. Felt experiences, personal relationships which are the most sacred of all, love outraged, friendship betrayed, trust broken, when we cry from the depths of our despair to know whether we live in a friendly world or have a friend on whom we can lean, when we sink into self-abasement and dark despair because we find no response from the universe; these are common to all human beings.

Films deal with ungovernable fits of temper or moodiness bordering on madness or triumphal expressions of joy and fulfilment. We find that we think one course is right but do the other. We are divided in our minds. Such cases of self-division, self-analysis, self-criticism and self-repair are to be met with the world over. Because they deal with such universal aspects, films have a universal appeal, whether we are in Africa or Asia or any other part of the world.

The affluent countries have a sense of frustration and fear. People live in fear, the fear of nuclear annihilation, where all the great arts and civilizations may be reduced to dust and ashes. They are afraid for the security of their children; they are afraid for the safety of unborn generations who may become victims of radiation fallouts. So wherever we go, we have fear of this nuclear cataclysm. We wish to ward it off. In advance countries also there is a feeling that all is not well with the world. It is essential for us to remove this basic fear which means radical insufficiency in human nature itself. So whether we deal with universal problems of human nature or national problems, or international ones, we find a need to regenerate ourselves.

Everyone says we are passing through a crisis. Crisis means a parting of the ways; it means a judgement that the way in which we are living is not adequate to the requirements of our age, a judgement that something more will have to happen. We should not believe that man is obliged to bow to the inevitable. There is no such thing as inevitability in human affairs which is sometimes traced to historical materialism or to logical determinism or to providential necessity. It is Shakespeare who told us, 'we are not villains by necessity; we are not fools by heavenly compulsion.'

There is no kind of necessity driving us to accept whatever comes to us as inevitable. Man is a free being. He has in him spirit, which is able to stand up against the forces of nature, against the forces of history. It is in that way, by asserting our will, by overcoming the difficulties that confront us, that we will be able to build something better for ourselves. We overlook spirit in us when we simply swim on the surface of life, drift from one event to another and are alienated from the source of our being. Man is not a thing among things or an object among objects. He is a subject. If he becomes conscious of his subjectivity or inwardness, he ceases to be a victim of nature. If it is a crisis, it is a crisis which calls upon man to accept the challenge and makes him feel that it is his paramount duty not to bow down to circumstances, to the reality as we find it, but to reshape it according to a different pattern altogether. That is the force which resides in the spirit of man. Man's spirit must be regarded as essentially free.

It was H. G. Wells who remarked that the whole of history seems to be a kind of race between education and castastrophe. Catastrophe will overtake us if we do not reeducate ourselves. Another writer recently said that man's history started with an act of disobedience, of non-conformity, and may end up with an act of obedience if we do not assert our dignity but merely acquiesce in the nature of what is given to us. People may believe that it is inevitable, that there is nothing more for us to do. If that kind of attitude overtakes an individual or a nation, then it means that we are helping the castastrophe to occur and are not trying to ward off the catastrophe.

We are, therefore, at a parting of the ways today, both in our domestic history and in the history of the world. Either we have to move forward or slip back. There is no such thing as standing still or marking time. If we do not move forward, we slip back into anarchy, into a way of life reminding us of the jungle; and the whole history of the world will be wound up.

So it is that the great artists who are using this powerful instrument of films have it in them to help humanity to bring about a moral and spiritual revolution. The revolutiuon is possible. All our film artists and all the great writers themselves are of the view that there is nothing which we have to accept as completely irreversible. We cannot put even our bodies in reverse gear. It is necessary for us to go on with what we think is right. It is possible for us to look upon the whole of humanity as one family. It is possible for us, if we do not listen to the doctrinaires who try to overthrow our native generosity; they are the people who tell us that race, nation, religion have got certain fundamental attitudes which we have to adopt. Neither racial bigotry nor national egotism nor religious frenzy is inescapable. We can overcome all these if we can train our people properly; and the great artists are the people who show us *the* human characters wrestling with destiny and fate and trying to assert their superiority over the force of cirumstances themselves.

There are no people in the world who are wicked. We may be unfortunate, but we are not wicked; so also nations. Great artists always tell us that if we had been in the position of the characters they describe we would not have behaved in any different manner. Therefore, judge not; have forbearance, have patience; we are sinners all. We can plant seeds of forbearance and understanding in hearts seething with hatred.

Powerful films kindle the light of love, the lamp of compassion, even in hearts grown old and cold. Even with regard to the great international conflicts which have divided the world and have harassed it for centuries even there what is necessary is a little understanding. 'If I have one prayer to make to God', said Galsworthy, 'it is this: give me the power to understand.' The artists, the film artists specially, who have such a powerful instrument in their hands, can help us to understand that it is not right for us to go back to the past. We have to advance into the future. In this great adventure of the human spirit, it is possible for them to help us to go forward.

Trustee Of Human Vision

Our press has been very generous, very useful and very serviceable so far as our activities are concerned. Every generation has its own particular problems. Once we had the problem of fighting for freedom from foreign domination. Now we have the problem of building a stable democracy — stable in both the economic and political senses of the term. That is what we are interested in and in this way also, the press has been very useful to us. Of course, they are not always friendly to the establishment. Why should they be? It is not necessary. If the establishment is in the wrong, they must point out that greater honesty in public life will bring about less tension and less friction and it is their duty to tell us where we go wrong and where we can check ourselves. That task also the press is discharging very satisfactorily but we cannot say that we do not have monopoly newspapers, we do not have yellow journalism.

There are people always interested in promoting their circulations by flaunting vice and scandals, sex and crime — such things are also here and it is, as has been already said, through a process of self-discipline that people can improve standards of journalism. Both the readers and the journalists themselves act and react and if they do not want to spoil the taste of the general public, they will have to exercise some restraint on themselves and raise standards of journalism.

At this particular moment, throughout the world, the central aim seems to be social equality and world peace. In other stages of history we wanted to get rich quick by harnessing the forces of nature, we wanted to gain spiritual enlightenment by undertaking exercises, etc., we wanted to win and conquer other people.

But today, almost all the people of the world are united in saying that the two things necessary are social equality and world unity and peace. Equality, you may say is not a fact; it is not the Law of Nature, we are born unequal and why do you want to equalize? The point is, the State has to provide equal opportunities for all people and enable them to develop. That is why there have been protest against racial segregation, political domination and economic exploitation. All these things we have been protesting against in the name of social equality.

So far as world peace is concerned, no country can thrive now without real peace. It is unfortunate that sometimes people do not communicate to their readers the gross dire consequences of any kind of nuclear conflict. I saw a film, the 'Game of War', reporting the way in which men, women and children are mutilated and thrown into a heap by the activities of nuclear weapons but I was told that the particular film was not intended to be shown to all. In other words, it is easy for us to stimulate the baser instincts of human nature. To develop the higher instincts requires some kind of exercise or discipline. Compassion and fellow-feeling, these are the qualities which we should develop. The world is changing much faster than we are able to change ourselves. We still resort to ancient methods of sovereign nationalism and military methods for settling our international disputes. We proclaim that we should all try to decide our issues, even international issues, by conciliation, by persuasion, negotiation and arbitration, by mutual understanding. That is what we have to do. That requires a real, ultimate change in human nature which newspaper editors and responsible men can bring about if they are honest to their profession, honest to the ideals of world peace, honest to the principles which they are advocating.

There are different ways in which social transformation can be brought about. We wish to bring about that social transformation by means of democratic processes and procedures. There are other people who wish to impose some particular system of thought — economic and political — in which they fervently believe. Still others use the phraseology of revolution and try to make themselves most important and use the whole community a servant of themselves. We have the democratic, the doctrinaire and the opportunist methods of bringing about social changes, human transformation, the transformation of human society. What we are interested in doing is to bring about a transformation of human beings, human society, through democratic processes and procedures. Even systems which adopt liberalism as an official creed are uprooted.

Sometimes a group of powerful men are able to dictate and subjugate the minds of millions of other people and determine their direction and purpose in life. There must be a real participation of the community in the making of decisions.

That is the meaning of true democracy. If we do not want to have any kind of doctrinaire transformation of society, if we do not want to have individuals get to the top by using society for their own ends, by using all the psychological methods of which we are in command today, we have to adopt democratic processes and that is what this country is pledged to.

The press has got a great responsibility. It is not the old, usual press today. Any man who joins the profession of journalism must have been grounded in some subject politics, economics, art, sport, agriculture, women's problems, whatever they may be, he must be a specialist in one particular field, at least in one particular field. We cannot be professionals in all things. It is a matter of regret that, after tape-recording came, shorthand is going down. I remember once giving a few lectures at Manchester University, the lecture was between five and six. By the time I went home, the reporter from the *Manchester*

Guardian came with report of my speech asking for corrections. I do not think that sort of thing prevails today.

Tape-recording has entailed a loss to the art of shorthand writing. There are many people, who join the profession of journalism, who are reporting in longhand what happens anywhere. Balance and proportion should be the ideals which each journalist should have before him. Without the qualities of proportion and balance, it is not possible to appeal to the larger numbers. We may appeal to a few people for a time, but the populace will judge according to the way in which we do these things.

We talk about a free press being a responsible press. Yes, responsibility is from within, responsibility is not imposed from without. If there is corrupt individualism, it has to be exposed, if there is an insane act of violence, you will have to denounce that as best as you can, if there is lack of restraint in the conduct of people, that must be exposed — these are things which a responsible editor is expected to do. He must not be bound by what is fashionable and what is not fashionable. He must find out what is true and what is in the best interests of the nation.

This country has had an international outlook from even the beginnings of the struggle for freedom. We owe it to Jawaharlal Nehru who made us have an international mind. He had opinions on these questions and his opinions were accepted by Gandhiji, who never claimed to be an expert or specialist in international affairs. But he trusted Jawharlal Nehru so that a political awareness of the problems that are agitating the world today is there innate in the minds of the Indian reader.

We must have more Asian and African news. We should have more European news, more world news. The world has become one, whether you like it or not, East and West have come together and they can never part again. It is, therefore, essential for us to understand what is happening in Vietnam, what is happening in Congo, what is happening in other parts of the world. Every individual is a trustee for the future of the world, is a trustee of human vision, of human responsibility. He has a sense of obligation to the whole world, to the future of humanity. He must develop a humanist vision of society a vision of society in which man is treated as a man and not as Greek or Barbarian, Catholic or Protestant, Arab or Jew, Hindu or Moslems; he must be treated as a human being. Nothing should be regarded as alien to any other human being.

